Nate the Great
and The
Hungry
Book
Club

by Marjorie Weinman Sharmat
and Mitchell Sharmat

illustrated by Jody Wheeler
in the style of Marc Simont

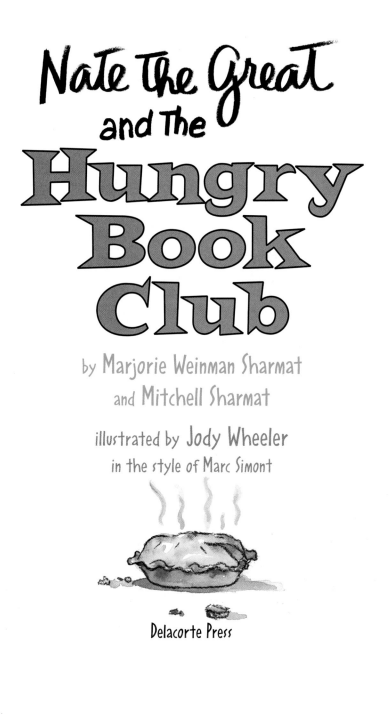

Delacorte Press

We want to thank the members of the Harvard Book Club of Southern Arizona for the inspiration they innocently and inadvertently provided for this book. —Marjorie Weinman Sharmat and Mitchell Sharmat

Text copyright © 2009 by Marjorie Weinman Sharmat and Mitchell Sharmat
New illustrations of Nate the Great, Sludge, Rosamond, Annie, Oliver, Pip, Finley, Claude, Esmeralda, Harry, Fang, and the Hexes by Jody Wheeler based upon the original drawings by Marc Simont. All other images copyright © 2009 by Jody Wheeler

Visit us on the Web! www.randomhouse.com/kids

Educators and librarians, for a variety of teaching tools, visit us at www.randomhouse.com/teachers

Library of Congress Cataloging-in-Publication Data is available upon request.
ISBN 978-0-385-73695-4 (hardcover)—ISBN 978-0-385-90637-1 (lib. bdg.)

The text of this book is set in 17-point Goudy.
Book design by Trish Parcell
Printed in the United States of America
10 9 8 7 6 5 4 3
First Edition

Remembering

my father, Nathan Weinman   NATE
my mother, Anna Weinman   ANNIE
my sister, Rosalind Weinman ROSAMOND
my uncle, Harry Weinman   HARRY
my dog, Fritz Melvin Sharmat SLUDGE

and you know them all
—M.W.S.

For Trombone Bruce Glasberg
—J.W.

Chapter One
Torn, Ripped, Ruined

My name is Nate the Great.
I am a detective.
My dog, Sludge, is a detective too.
"Ouch!"
Right now I am a mumbling, bumbling,
tripping detective.
I have just tripped over
a big pile of books
that Rosamond left in my house.

Sludge is sniffing them.
He has been sniffing them
since Rosamond knocked on my door
this morning.
She was carrying a bunch of books.
Three more were piled on her head.
Rosamond looked very strange.
Rosamond looks strange all the time.
"I have great news," she said.
"I have started a book club.
I am calling it Rosamond's Ready Readers.
But there is trouble in the club.
One of the members is trying
to wreck my cookbook. Look!"
Rosamond took a book off her head.
The other two books fell off.
"Why are you carrying books on top
of your head?" I asked.
"Because I'm president of a club now.

These books help me hold my head high
and look like a president."
I, Nate the Great, knew that I was
looking at a very strange president.

"This is my new cookbook," she said.
"Yesterday I left it open on my
kitchen table after I made treats
for the club meeting.
When the meeting was over,
I went to get the treats
for the members.
The page that was open
was torn, ripped, *ruined!*"
Sludge and I looked at the page.
I, Nate the Great, say that
it was torn, ripped, ruined.

Chapter Two
The Crime Scene

Rosamond pulled something out of
her pocket.

"Here is a photo of the crime scene,"
she said.

I looked at the photo. "Your kitchen
was a crime scene?"

"Of course. Keep this photo and study it.
You can see that my cookbook
is in the middle of my huge, high table.

The torn page had a recipe for tuna fish pie.
The bits of pie that fell
on the page are gone too.
I want you to find the evil monster
who did this!"
"Monster?"
"Yes. The Evil Page Monster,"
Rosamond said.

"Now, here is my plan. The next meeting
will be at my house this afternoon.
You and Sludge can come undercover.
Just pretend you are new members.
I'll be using this cookbook again.
Meanwhile, I'll leave these other
books here, where they'll be safe.
I left one book at home.
The members will be reading it
at today's meeting."
Rosamond piled her books on my floor.
"You are so lucky to have this case!"

I, Nate the Great, did not agree.
"Perhaps this is a case for a bookworm,"
I said.
"Enjoy being a bookworm," Rosamond said.
I looked at Sludge.
We both knew that if I didn't take the case,
Rosamond would come back.
And back. And back.
And back.

Chapter Three
A Book Case

I wrote a note to my mother.

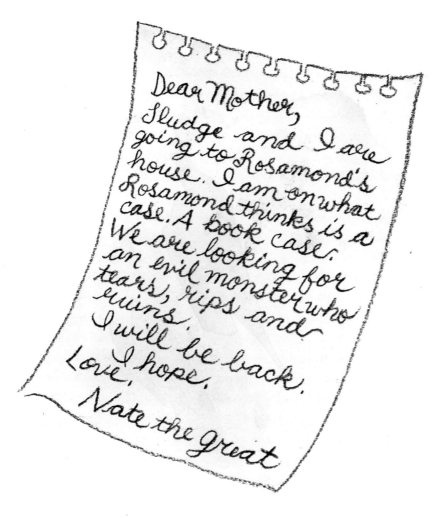

Dear Mother,
Sludge and I are
going to Rosamond's
house. I am on what
Rosamond thinks is a
case. A book case.
We are looking for
an evil monster who
tears, rips and
ruins.
I will be back,
I hope,
Love,
Nate the Great

Chapter Four
The Hungry Book Club

It was afternoon.

Sludge and I went to Rosamond's house.

She answered the door.

She had only one book on her head.

I peered inside her house.

I saw Oliver, Pip, Finley, Claude,
Esmeralda, Annie, and Annie's little
brother, Harry, sitting in a circle.

Also sitting in the circle were Annie's
dog, Fang, and Rosamond's four cats,
Plain Hex, Little Hex, Big Hex,
and Super Hex.

I stepped back. "The Hexes and Fang
belong to your book club?"
"Sure," Rosamond said.
"Everybody loves stories.
And treats. I serve tuna fish pie to the
cats and meat patties to Fang.
Everybody else gets cookies.

This is a very hungry book club.
Come in."
"I, Nate the Great, am not in the mood
for cookies or circles," I said.
"Sludge and I will sit in a corner."

Chapter Five
Meet Harvard Hedgehog

Rosamond sat down in a big chair.
She took the book off her head.
She held it up.
"This is our book for today,"
she announced.
"*Harvard Hedgehog*.
We will take turns reading it out loud.
Then we will talk about the book.
I will start.

'Harvard Hedgehog was always late.
He arrived at parties just in time
to bump into everyone leaving.
He nibbled leftover cake crumbs
and lapped melted ice cream.
Then he sat in a corner
and exclaimed, "Wonderful party!"
to the empty room.'"

I, Nate the Great, was sitting in a corner
like Harvard Hedgehog.
I pretended to go to sleep.
But I was watching, watching.
The book went from member to member.
Nobody was tearing pages.
It was Esmeralda's turn to read.

"'When Harvard went to the movies,
he always got there
when the movie was over.
As everyone was going out,
Harvard was going in.
He would sit down on stale popcorn
and look up at the big, empty screen.
"Great show!" he exclaimed to no one.
Harvard meant to be on time,
but he never was. . . .'"

Suddenly Esmeralda stopped reading.
She looked puzzled.
"A page is missing," she said.
Rosamond looked straight at me.
"A ripped page in one book
and now a missing page from another.
When I bought this book,
there were no pages missing.
I know because I read the entire book
before I bought it!"
I, Nate the Great, looked at Sludge.
I now knew we had a real case.

Chapter Six
Double Trouble

Rosamond raised her arms.
"As president of Rosamond's Ready
Readers, I will not let this stop
our book club meeting.
Members, who would like to tell me
what you think of the book so far?"
Esmeralda raised her hand. "At first I
thought that Harvard needed a watch,
but now I know he needs a page."

Claude raised his hand.
Claude was always losing things.
"I don't like the book
because Harvard doesn't lose anything,"
he said. "If you never lose anything,
you never have a chance to find
what you didn't lose."
"Excellent thought," Rosamond said.

Oliver spoke up. "I follow people.
Everyone knows I do.
Harvard doesn't
follow anybody. Harvard is
a very boring hedgehog."

"Thank you for sharing that with us,"
Rosamond said.

"Me, me, me!" Harry was
jumping up and down.
"I like the book.
I like the picture of
Harvard smiling in front of
the big clock the best."

Rosamond smiled.
"Well, we have a nice happy Harvard,
and a happy Harry," she said.

"I am proud of all my members.
Except whoever ripped a page
and took a page."

I, Nate the Great, was thi
Who would rip
a page of the cookbook and
take a page of *Harvard Hed*
Someone who liked the boo
or someone who disliked the
Or someone who couldn't decide?
And where was the missing page?
"I would like to see the book," I said.

Rosamond handed it to me.
"I see that the missing page
would have been numbered 15 on one side
and 16 on the other," I said.
"Numbers, crumbers," Rosamond said.
"You have a double mystery.
Just solve it!"

Chapter Seven
The Evil
Page Monster

Rosamond stood up.
"Now it's time for treats," she said.
"The animals are getting restless."
Sludge and I followed Rosamond
to the kitchen.
It was a mess.
But Sludge sniffed and sniffed.
He liked this case
because it smelled good.
I saw a cookbook on the table.

This time the book was open
to a recipe for meat patties.
There were bits of meat on the page.
Rosamond must have been using the
cookbook today to make her treats.
This page had no rips.
Hmmm.

Fang and the Hexes walked in.
Fang sniffed the table.
He started to jump up
and reach for the cookbook.
"Stop!" Rosamond yelled.
"You, Fang, are the Evil Page Monster!

I, President Rosamond,
have solved this case.
Fang must have sneaked in
during yesterday's meeting,
eaten the bits of food,
and ripped the page.
And now I've stopped him
from doing it again."
Rosamond folded her arms
and looked at me.
"Time to find the missing page," she said.
I, Nate the Great, had two choices.
I could search for the missing page
or I could go home and eat pancakes
and think.

Chapter Eight
Sniffs

I ate my pancakes
while Sludge ate a bone.
Then Sludge walked around the room.
He was looking for something.
And he found it.
It was the photo Rosamond had left here.
He sniffed it and sniffed it and sniffed it.
Was he trying to tell me something?

Was the ripped-page case really solved?
Did Fang really do it?
I looked at the photo again.
The page in the cookbook
had no food on it.
The page I had seen at Rosamond's house
had tiny bits of meat on it.

The recipe in the photo was for
tuna fish pie.
The recipe at her house was for
meat patties.
One recipe for cats, one recipe for dogs.
"Good work, Sludge," I said.

Chapter Nine
Not So Fast

I called Rosamond.
"I am coming back to your house," I said.
"And I need Annie and Fang to be there."
I put the photo of the tuna fish pie page
in my pocket.

Sludge and I rushed to Rosamond's house.
Rosamond was waiting for us at the door.
"Your ripped-page case is not solved,"
I said.

"That fangy Fang did it!" Rosamond said.
"And here he comes down the street
with Annie."
"We must all go into the kitchen," I said.
Rosamond, Annie, Fang, Sludge, and I
went into the kitchen.
The cookbook was still open on the table.
Fang sniffed and ran to the table.
"Ho hum," Rosamond said. "We already
know that Fang ripped a page yesterday."

"Wait!" I said.

Fang jumped up and put his front paws
on the table.

He opened his jaws.

He stretched.

But he couldn't reach the cookbook.

"This table is too high and big for Fang,"
I said.

"Poor Fang," Annie said. "He's big
and smart, but he isn't that stretchy."

I, Nate the Great, already knew that.
Fang would have grabbed the bits of meat
during the meeting
if he could have reached them!
Rosamond sighed. "Okay, so Fang
couldn't have ripped the page yesterday."
"Correct," I said. "Also, he doesn't
like tuna fish pie."
I pulled the cookbook photo out of
my pocket.

"This photo shows the cookbook open
to a tuna fish pie recipe. But the open
pages have no bits of tuna fish on them."
"I already knew that," Rosamond said.
"I, Nate the Great, say that someone
reached for those tuna fish bits
and was scratching and tearing
to get every last bit."
"Who?" Rosamond asked.

"Little Hex," I said. "He can leap high.
Also, he can hide in small spaces.
He is so small that he could have
gone into the kitchen and come back
without your seeing him."
Rosamond clapped her hands.
"Little Hex is growing up!
My darling little Page Monster."
"I, Nate the Great, say that
the ripped-page case is solved.
And you should try to keep your
kitchen neater.
Clean clues are better."
I took two bones from my pocket
and gave one to Fang and one to Sludge.
Rosamond kept clapping.
"Little Hex must have taken the
Harvard Hedgehog page too.
What a talent he has!"
"Not so fast," I said.

"You are trying to reuse a clue.
Little Hex might not have taken
the page.
Tell me everything about
your *Harvard Hedgehog* book."
"Well, yesterday Annie and I went to the
book sale at the school around the corner.
I bought the book there.
I read it before I bought it.
There weren't any missing pages.
After I bought the book,
I kept it with me.
In my hands. On my head.

I even slept with it."
"Is there anything else
I should know?" I asked.
"No. I'm a president. I think
of everything."
"Then I must leave," I said.
"Leave? But you just came."
"That's how it is
in the detective business," I said.
"We come. We go.
We go where the clues take us."
I, Nate the Great, knew that
I needed more clues.
If the book was with Rosamond
all the time,
how could a page be missing?

BOOK SALE
TODAY
9-5

Chapter Ten
Stretchy Fang

Annie, Fang, Sludge, and I left
Rosamond's house.
"I am looking for a new clue,"
I said to Annie. "A missing-page clue."
"I don't have any clue," Annie said.
"But I want you to know
that Fang can be stretchy
some of the time. You should have
seen him at the school book sale."

"What?" I said. "He was there?"
"I brought him along when
I went with Rosamond," Annie said.
"Tell me exactly how
Fang was stretchy there," I said.
"Well, we went to the Used Books table.
A lady there told us that some books
might have food stains,
loose bindings, and faded pages.
Rosamond began picking through books
and reading them.
If she liked a book, she put it in a pile
on the table.
Suddenly Fang put his paws on the table
and started to sniff a book.
There were stains on it
that looked like
chicken noodle soup.
Fang licked the book.

Then he pawed through
more books and licked pages.
Lots of books fell to the floor.
Fang was really stretchy.
It was his kind of table."

"Then what happened?"
"I picked up the books that
Fang had licked and I bought them.
Rosamond's pile had toppled over,
but she scooped up her books
from the table and the floor
and bought them.

We both went home with full bags.
Since Fang had licked and liked the
books, I put them all in his doghouse."
"Thank you for the information," I said.
I turned to Sludge.
"You and I are going to school!"

Chapter Eleven
School Clues

Sludge and I rushed to the school.
The book sale was in the gym.
A lady walked up to us.
I knew she was a librarian because
she had a badge on her shirt that said
LIBRARIAN.
Sometimes being a detective is easy.

"Hello," I said. "I am looking for
Harvard Hedgehog."
"You're in luck," the librarian said.
"We've sold two copies of *Harvard,*
but we still have one left.
And here he is on the table."
"Do you have pages 15 and 16?" I asked.
"Yes. The pages are in good shape.
Clean, and with strong binding."

"No chicken noodle soup?" I said.
"What?"
"I was just thinking.
I'm a detective.
I think a lot.
I think I will buy this book."
I bought the book and thanked
the librarian.
Then Sludge and I went home.

Chapter Twelve
The Hedgehog Picture

I sat down in my favorite chair.
I opened my *Harvard Hedgehog* book.
I turned to page 15.
There was a picture of Harvard
getting his photo taken
in front of a big clock.

He looked proud. And he was smiling.
But why would anyone take *that* page?
I, Nate the Great, say that
there must be far better things
in this world to watch
than a hedgehog posing for his photo.
And then I remembered something.
What I had just seen
in the book was not news to me.
I had already heard about it.
I, Nate the Great, was about
to solve this case.

Chapter Thirteen
Reading Together

I had two clues.
School clues.
I was told that the pages
in my book were in good shape.
Clean. Strong binding.
Annie was told that some books
had loose bindings.
Hmmm. Pages. Bindings.

I, Nate the Great, say that a loose binding
could cause a loose page,
and a loose page could become
a missing page.
There had been three copies of the
Harvard Hedgehog book at the
Used Books table.

Rosamond had picked a good copy.
But when her pile fell down,
she must have grabbed the copy
that had the missing page.
She didn't know it.
Annie must have bought the good copy
that Rosamond had picked out,
and she didn't know it.

And how did I, Nate the Great, know it?
Because I now remembered where I had
heard about Harvard Hedgehog smiling in
front of a big clock.
From Harry! At the book club meeting.
But how could Harry have known
what was on page 15, since it was missing?
Because he had seen the book at home!
Harry must have been looking
at Fang's books.
And he saw the Harvard Hedgehog picture.

I turned to Sludge.
"I must give this book to Rosamond
and tell her that the case is solved.
I must also tell Annie to feed Fang
plenty of chicken noodle soup.

But there is something else
I want to do first."
I, Nate the Great, picked up every book
that Rosamond had brought over
and carefully put them on a shelf.
"Just where they should be," I said.

Then I took my *Harvard Hedgehog* book
and sat down in my chair.
"I am going to read this book
as a reader and not
as a detective," I said.
"Let's read it together."
Sludge jumped up on my lap.
And I, Nate the Great, read and read
until I reached . . .